D087420B

HELLO HEDDY LEVI!

illustrations by
Harvey Klineman

HELLO HEDDY LEVI!

by
Yaffa Ganz

FELDHEIM PUBLISHERS
Jerusalem ● New York

A glossary of Hebrew and Yiddish words appears
at the end of this book.

First published 1989

Copyright © 1989
Yaffa Ganz

Philipp Feldheim Inc.   Feldheim Publishers Ltd
200 Airport Executive Park   POB 6525/Jerusalem, Israel
Spring Valley, NY 10977

Library of Congress Cataloging-in-Publication Data

Ganz, Yaffa
Hello Heddy Levi!

Summary: Follows the adventures, at school and at home, of eleven-
year-old Heddy Levi, the youngest, smartest, and most original girl in
the eighth-grade class at Karem Hatorah Yeshiva.
[1. Jews — Fiction.   2. Schools — Fiction]
I. Klineman, Harvey, ill.   II. Title.
PZ7.G1537He 1988 [Fic] 88-30997
ISBN 0-87306-480-1

Printed in Israel

To Shani,
who is a blessing and a joy,
and to her Abba,
who is very special indeed.

contents

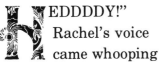

a walk in the rain

HEDDDDY!" Rachel's voice came whooping through the closed windows all the way up to the second floor.

"HEDDY! Are you sleeping? Come on down!"

Heddy fumbled with the catch. She pushed the window up and caught a spray of freezing rain right in her face.

"Come on down!" Rachel called again. "It's too delicious to stay in!"

Heddy didn't know what was so delicious about a damp, dreary drizzle, but anything was better than staying alone in the house the rest of the afternoon. Now that Jeremy and Ezra were learning in a *yeshiva* out-of-town and Mom had started teaching piano in the music conservatory in the afternoons, there wasn't a soul around until suppertime. Even Zeidy had moved away to *Eretz Yisrael*, and Danny, her oldest brother, had gone with him for a year of studying. The house was so quiet that Heddy had actually fallen asleep in the middle of doing her homework! To make things even worse, the doctor told her not to go out in the sun for a few days, so maybe a walk in the rain was just what she needed.

"I'll be right down!" she called, struggling to shut the window. "Don't go away!" She grabbed her raincoat and rainhat and zoomed (in a very unladylike manner) down the stairs to meet Rachel.

Rachel Travis was Heddy's First Best Friend. Heddy had several other best friends too, but she and Rachel had been First Best Friends ever since they were born. Their brothers, Jeremy and Sammy, were also best friends, and Heddy and Rachel were anxious to keep up the family tradition.

This year, Heddy was put up another grade in Kerem HaTorah Yeshiva. Only eleven years old, she was the youngest girl in the eighth class. In school, Mrs. Kramer called her Chedva, which always made her feel and act a little older and more mature. But back home, she was just plain Heddy again, as breathless and disorganized as ever. And to prove it, just as she was about to come out of the house, she turned around and ran back in.

"What's taking you so long?" Rachel called impatiently.

"I can't find my boots!" Heddy yelled back.

Heddy finally reappeared, still pulling on her boots. She closed the door to the house, kissed the mezuza and skipped down the stairs.

"Did you remember to lock the door?" asked Rachel.

"You bet! All I need is to leave the door unlocked again after I left it open twice last week! Even *I'm* not *that* scatterbrained!"

"What do you need your boots for?" Rachel moved the umbrella over Heddy's head. "I have an umbrella, and it's not raining that hard."

"I like to slosh through the water," said Heddy. "And when it's dark and cloudy, no one can see me and tell me I'm too old for puddles."

"You'll never be too old for puddles." Rachel smiled knowingly.

"Don't sound so high and mighty just because you're a few months older than I am," Heddy sniffed.

"Ten, to be exact," was Rachel's reply. "But let's not argue again. We argued enough yesterday."

"That was *your* fault, not mine," Heddy insisted. "Next time don't call me teacher's pet. I can't help it if I'm smart!"

"That's true," Rachel replied, "but you don't have to be so showy about it! Especially when we just finished learning about Moshe Rabbeinu and the importance of being modest and humble!"

Heddy was about to reply, but she changed her mind. Rachel was right. Sometimes she *did* show off a little. But she wasn't showy now. In fact, she was sort of hiding.

Rachel changed the subject. "What did the doctor tell you this morning? Your face doesn't look so good."

"So good? It looks perfectly horrible! The results came back from the laboratory. I'm allergic!"

"That's not *so* bad," Rachel said. "My brother is allergic too. It's better than being sick. What are you allergic to?"

Heddy shook her head. "You won't believe me."

"How do you know if you don't tell me?"

Heddy gulped. "To chocolate!"

Rachel was so surprised that she walked right into a puddle herself.

"Chocolate? How awful! Can't you eat *any*? *Ever*? What will you do at the chocolate party next Wednesday?"

"My mother says I'll have to persevere, whatever that means. My father says I'll survive, and the doctor says he's sure I'll manage! How does he know? You'd think it was the easiest thing in the world not to eat chocolate! Well, it's not. I'd rather eat chocolate than anything else. And every time I eat some, two hours later I'm red as a beet, swollen as a pumpkin, and itchy as a burlap bag! The doctor even told me not to go out in the sun until the allergy calms down. Not that I'd go outside in the light looking like this!" Heddy did look rather red and bumpy.

"Don't worry, Heddy," Rachel consoled her. "Life is full of problems. My sister told me so. You're supposed to say *gam zu letova* when trouble comes your way. But an allergy isn't really so terrible. It'll go

away by tomorrow, and no one will see you in the rain today. And it's lots better than being covered with paint. *That* took a week to come off!"

Heddy groaned. "Don't remind me," she said. Last Pesach she had walked around with purple eyebrows, purple hair and purple skin spots. All she had wanted was to make a pretty purple design on the ceiling of her bedroom to match her new purple bedspreads, but like so many other things in Heddy's life, it hadn't quite work out as planned.

"The rain is wonderful," said Rachel, shaking a drop off the tip of her nose. "Did you know that the seas and oceans and rivers evaporate and come falling down again in tiny drops — all pure and clean — so that everything can live and be healthy and grow?"

"Everyone knows that!" Heddy stopped for a moment. "Do you think the rain might be able to help a blotchy face?"

"Who knows? Maybe. Rain is like a miracle. There should be a special *bracha* for rain!"

"And one for puddles," added Heddy with a grin.

The two girls laughed, and arm in arm, they sloshed their way through several middle-sized puddles, shaking the rain from the drippy trees onto Rachel's umbrella and thoroughly enjoying their watery afternoon stroll. It *was* a rather delicious day, thought Heddy. And maybe the rain would wash some of her chocolate allergy away after all.

a gift for Zeidy

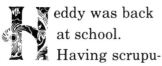eddy was back at school. Having scrupulously removed every drop of chocolate from her diet, she felt allergy-safe and happy. It wasn't even so bad, once she explained it to all her friends. They prepared vanilla candy and cookies for the chocolate party, and Jeremy and Ezra sent her two dozen bags of carob candy from New York.

"It's made from a carob tree and it's supposed to taste like chocolate," Jeremy explained in their letter. "Shimon bar Yochai ate the fruit from a carob tree all the years he was hiding from the Romans. He became a great *talmid chacham*. Maybe the carob candy will make you smarter too. On second thought, maybe that's not such a good idea. If you get any smarter, they'll put you ahead a few more grades and you'll graduate high school before you finish the eighth grade!"

Heddy smiled as she read the letter. Poor Jeremy! Ever since she broke the secret code he and Sammy Travis had made up in the sixth grade, he thought she was some kind of a genius!

She wished Jeremy and Ezra could have found a yeshiva closer to home. She was glad she finally had a bedroom to herself, but the house seemed so empty. There was hardly a soul around to argue with. Then Zeidy and Danny left too, and Heddy missed them all.

Well, at least she hadn't forgotten Zeidy's birthday. Dad had sent the package out this morning. It was a rather unusual gift, but she felt it was just the right thing.

The phone rang. As usual, it was Rachel. Heddy sat back on a nice, soft chair and settled down for their daily after-school conversation.

Rachel? Hi! What's new? No, I can't go shopping or spend any money now...

I can't spend any because I don't have any. I spent it all on a birthday present for my grandfather...

I bought him (Heddy hesitated for a moment) — *a pair of long underwear...*

You heard me. Long winter underwear...

What do you mean "What kind of a gift is that"? What's wrong with it?...

A more normal gift? Like what? WHAT? A box of candy??? What would Zeidy do with a box of candy? He doesn't eat candy...

How could I possibly send a cake to Israel? And

how could I possibly get seventy candles on a cake?...

FLOWERS? For a Zeidy? Don't be ridiculous...

He doesn't wear a belt. He wears suspenders...

He doesn't need a cigarette lighter. He doesn't smoke...

He doesn't need a book. He has around three thousand sefarim. *And anyway, I asked my Mom and she said he needs long underwear for the cold winters in Jerusalem. So I bought it. What's so terrible about long underwear? They were the deluxe model! And every time it's cold, Zeidy will put them on and feel warmer and he'll think of me...*

I don't have to give Zeidy glamorous gifts. He's a very practical person and he likes practical gifts. Remember what he gave me last year? A tool box, so I wouldn't have to take Jeremy's tools all the time. It's the most useful gift I ever got. Even Mom borrows my screwdriver when her sewing maching starts jumping around...

Okay, okay, I promise not to buy you long underwear for YOUR birthday. Just do me a favor, will you? When MY birthday comes around, don't buy me any either!

two
for the zoo

eddy stuck her head out of the window once more to check the weather. It was still beautiful — warm, sunny, dry and not a cloud to be seen. "Perfect zoo weather!" she said to herself.

Heddy and Aviva were taking the twins to the zoo. The "Twins", as they were known, were Shuli and Shlomi Langsner. They were Aviva's next door neighbors. Five years old, perfectly adorable, and never a dull moment when they're around. That's what their babysitters said. When Mrs. Langsner had asked Aviva to watch them Sunday afternoon, Aviva called Heddy and asked for reinforcements.

"I can manage them alone in their house for an hour or two, but I'm not willing to take a chance on a whole afternoon all by myself! Two are really too much for one unarmed babysitter!"

"No problem," Heddy proclaimed confidently. "We'll take them where they can't do any harm. I know! Let's go to the zoo and we'll have a ball."

Heddy was going to meet Aviva at the Langsner's house, but first she checked her equipment: purse, money, keys, tissues, lunch, candy, fruit, and Mom's pretty straw hat for the sun.

"Remember, Heddy," Mom had said, "I want it back in the same condition I'm giving it to you!"

"Don't worry, Mom. I'm not going to eat it!"

"I know you're not," said her mother. "I was thinking about the Twins!"

"They aren't *that* bad, Mom. Besides, they'll have plenty of other stuff to eat. We're bringing enough food for three days of picnics, plus whatever their mother is sending."

"Are you *sure* you and Aviva can manage them? It's a big responsibility to take those two! Maybe you should just stay in our back yard and play with them."

"Don't be silly, Mom. I'm not a baby! And how much trouble can two little kids be? It'll be fine!" Heddy kissed her mother goodbye. "I'll be back by six. 'Bye!"

Heddy found Aviva and The Twins ready and waiting. They looked charming — bright and clean, with curly brown hair, sparkling blue eyes, and round rosy cheeks. Heddy smiled every time she looked at them.

"Do we have everything? Good! Let's go!" Aviva took Shlomi, Heddy took Shuli and they were off.

"I don't know what my mother was so worried about," said Heddy. "They're behaving like two angels."

"Keep your eyes on them anyway!" answered Aviva.

"I am! But why are you so nervous? Look at them watching the flamingoes! Aren't they cute?"

"Who? The flamingoes?"

"No!" said Heddy. "The Twins!"

"Oops, watch out! Here they come!" said Aviva.

"What do you want, Shuli?" Heddy asked. "My hat? But you have your own hat!"

"Yours is bigger. The sun comes through mine and I'm hot!"

"Yours is big enough for you. This is my mother's hat. I can't give it to you."

"But I'm hot! I wanna go home and get a bigger hat!"

"Look at the pretty flamingoes! They don't have a hat!"

"I don't care. I wanna go home to get another hat!"

"Can't you let her wear the hat for a few minutes?" asked Aviva. "What can she do to it? Otherwise we'll have her screaming for the next half hour."

"I guess so," said Heddy hesitantly.

She put the wide straw hat carefully on Shuli's head and tied it down tightly. "Now don't touch it,

Shuli, or it might fall off. It's big on you."

Shuli smiled her charming smile and went back to the fence to watch the flamingoes.

The next thing Heddy knew, she saw a lovely, wide, blue straw hat flying over the fence and PLOP! right onto a large wet rock in the flamingo pond.

"Shuli!!! What did you do!"

"You said the flamingoes didn't have a hat, so I gave them yours. Will they be cooler now, Heddy?"

Heddy felt a big slap growing on the tip of her hand, but she clenched her fist and held it tightly in. "Hold onto her while I try and retrieve my hat," she told Aviva.

She took off her shoes and socks and climbed carefully over the low fence. Then she waded into the flamingo pool to get the hat. On the way, she slipped.

"Hey, girlie! This isn't a swimming pool! Get out of there!" It was one of the zoo guards.

"Oh oh! Uh...my hat...it blew in...I just wanted to get it out."

"Then hurry up and get it out! And get yourself out as well! And don't go climbing into the animals' quarters again! If you have any problems, call one of the keepers!"

Heddy hurried over the fence so quickly that she caught the hem of her skirt and it ripped.

"Boy, do you look like a mess," said Aviva surveying the dripping Heddy and the torn skirt. "Let's sit in the sun awhile and dry you off. And here, I have a few safety pins. You can pin up your skirt. At least nothing happened to your mother's hat!"

"Heddy, I want to ride the elephant!" said Shlomi suddenly.

"Impossible!" answered Heddy firmly. "It's not allowed."

"But Mommy said we would have a good time at the zoo, and if I can't ride the elephant, I can't have a good time."

"I have a wonderful idea," Aviva interrupted. "Let's go feed the monkeys. See, we have a bagful of peanuts!"

"I have to go to the bathroom," Shuli said.

"Oy! The bathrooms are way back at the beginning of the zoo. Can't you wait?"

"No! I have to go NOW!"

"I don't wanna go to the bathrooms," Shlomi began to cry. "We already went there. I want to feed the monkeys. And if we don't go there, I want to go ride on the elephants!"

"Listen," said Heddy hurriedly. "You take him to the monkeys and I'll take her to the bathroom and I'll meet you at the picnic area near the merry-go-round. We can eat lunch on the grass there."

"Let's buy some soda first," said Shuli on the way to the bathroom.

Heddy sighed. "I don't have my money here.

Aviva has it with the lunch bags. Besides, I thought you had to go to the bathroom."

"I do, but Mommy always says to drink first and go to the bathroom afterwards."

"Well, this time you can go to the bathroom first and drink later!"

Twenty long minutes later, Heddy and Shuli were finally back at the picnic area near the merry-go-round.

"Can we have a ride? Please?" asked Shlomi.

"After we eat," said Aviva.

"I throw up if I ride the merry-go-round after I eat," said Shlomi.

"But I get sick if I ride on an empty stomach," said Shuli.

"Okay, okay! Aviva will take Shlomi now and I'll take Shuli after lunch," said an exasperated Heddy.

"I *told* you they're a handful," groaned Aviva.

"Don't complain," said Heddy. "Nothing dreadful has happened so far. And we can rest a little after lunch. Aren't we lucky it's not crowded today? It's nice and quiet."

"*Too* quiet," said Aviva. "Where's Shlomi?"

Heddy sat up and looked around. Shuli was playing peacefully in the sand. Shlomi was no where to be seen.

"Shuli, where is Shlomi?"

"He went to the lions."

"What? All by himself? When?"

"I don't know. He said he wants to see the lions and he can't wait for you."

The girls hurried to put their things together and get over to the lions.

"Come *on*, Shuli. We're going."

"No. I like it here in the sand. I don't like lions."

"Come on, Shuli! Now!!!" Shuli made a face, but she stood up in the sandpile and came towards Heddy and Aviva.

Suddenly a loud roar echoed through the zoo. Several more louder-still roars followed. It seemed as if all the lions were shouting at once.

"Oh my goodness! Shlomi! What's he into now!?"

Heddy grabbed Shuli and the girls started running. From far they already saw all the people, lined up in front of the lions' cages, watching. They gulped. There, inside one of the cages was a little boy with curly brown hair and a *kippa* on his head!

"Oh, excuse me...let me through...please. That's our baby...I mean, we're his babysitters."

"Hiya, Heddy! Hiya, Aviva! Look at me! I'm feeding the lions!"

Heddy was beside herself. She hardly understood when Aviva kept pulling her arm and saying, "It's okay, Heddy. The lions are locked up in the other cage. See? The keepers are inside the cage with Shlomi. Don't you see? It's okay!"

After that, all Heddy wanted to do was go home. She held Shlomi so tightly on the bus that he complained she was "squashing" him.

"I didn't have a good time at all," cried Shlomi. "You didn't let me ride the elephant and you made me come out of the lions' cage!"

"I didn't have a good time, either," complained Shuli. "I never got any soda and I couldn't finish my sandcastle."

They handed the children over to Mrs. Langsner with a sigh of relief. "How was it?" she asked smilingly.

"We wanna go to the zoo with Heddy and Aviva again!" they both cried. "Shlomi went into the lions' cage and Heddy went swimming with the flamingoes!"

Mrs. Langsner smiled understandingly as she paid the girls. "Would you like to watch them again next Sunday?"

"Uh...I don't think so, Mrs. Langsner," Heddy answered quickly. "I think I have to practice the piano next Sunday. In fact I'm *sure* of it. But thanks for asking. 'Bye!"

Mrs. Levi examined her hat carefully. "Well, it doesn't seem to be damaged any, and it's easy enough to fix the hem on your dress, so all in all, I guess the day didn't turn out too badly."

"Ouch!" cried Heddy, as she stuck her finger for the fourth time. "It's easy enough for *you* to fix the hem on my dress, but it's not so easy for *me!*"

"The trouble with you, Heddy, is that you don't concentrate on what you're doing!"

"I *am* concentrating, Mom. But I'm doing two things at once. I'm sewing and I'm thinking, and I'm concentrating on the thinking part now."

"Not even angels can do two things at once," said Mom, taking the dress from Heddy. "What are you so busy thinking about?"

"Well, at first I thought that babysitting would be a cinch. Then I discovered it wasn't so cinchy. I guess even easy-looking things can be hard to do. Those twins took an awful lot of patience out of me. In fact, I doubt if I have any left!"

Mom just laughed. "Don't worry about it. Patience grows back, and each time you use it up, you get a little more the next time round. Here's your dress. Next time you wear it, remember — you're too big to go swimming with flamingoes!"

"Thanks, Mom! But there's one thing I'll never be too big for... *this*!" And she promptly gave her mother a large hug.

playing the part

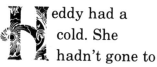**H**eddy had a cold. She hadn't gone to school that morning. Now she was lying in bed doing a puzzle when the phone rang. She picked it up.

"Heddy? Is it you? It's me, Rachel. Guess what? Mrs. Kramer chose you for the part of Nevuchadnezzar! Isn't that great? You're so lucky!"

Heddy was quiet. Was it great? She wasn't sure. She would much rather have been one of the Jews in the play. Or one of the good Babylonians. But the evil king???

"Well, aren't you excited?" Rachel asked. "It's the best part in the play."

"It is? Why?"

"Because Nevuchadnezzar gets to do the most interesting things. He makes long speeches and works himself up into a real furor over the Jews. Everyone hates him to pieces. You'll be great doing that!"

"Oh," she gulped, "I will?" Heddy's eyes filled with tears.

"Well, I gotta go now. See you tomorrow in school. 'Bye."

As Heddy put the phone down, Mom walked by her room and looked in. "Is something wrong, Heddy?"

"I guess not. That is, I'm not sure. Mrs. Kramer gave out the parts for the play. She wants me to be Nevuchadnezzar."

"That's a big part, isn't it?"

"Yes, I guess so."

"Then why do you sound so unhappy?"

"Well, would *you* like to be an evil king, destroyer of the *Beit Hamikdash*, enemy of the Jews? Nevuchadnezzar was just dreadful!"

"But it's only a play, Heddy, and someone has to be the king."

"Why can't it be someone else? Why me?"

"Well, it's your decision, dear, but it seems to me that it's an honor to get one of the main parts in the play. It means they think you can do a good job. You can help make the play a success so we make a lot of money for the school library."

Heddy didn't look convinced. "I'll think about it," was all she said.

By the next morning, Heddy had decided to try. But after two weeks of rehearsals, when everyone in school was calling her "Hedvuchadnezzar", she changed her mind.

"We're only kidding," said Aviva. "We didn't

mean anything by it."

"I don't care. I don't want to be the king."

"Don't be such a spoilsport, Heddy," said Terry. "If you quit now, you'll ruin everything. There's no one else to take your part."

"There is too. Anyone can do it. I'll be one of the Jews."

"No one else can do it like *you*!" said Rachel.

"I don't care. I won't be the king."

"I'm your First Assistant," said Miriam. "I'm an evil Babylonian too, and I'm not quitting!"

"So what? I am!"

"Well don't! You're acting like a baby!"

"What do you expect?" said someone else. "Maybe she *is* a baby! They skipped her twice. Maybe she's too young to know how to cooperate in eighth grade!"

"Girls, girls, enough!" Mrs. Kramer had walked into the auditorium and she looked very upset. "Rehearsal is over for today. Chedva, would you come into the office for a moment?"

Heddy would much rather have just gone home, straight to Mom for a good cry, but she couldn't very well do that now. So she picked her head up proud and tall and walked into the school office as if she didn't have a care in the world.

"Sit down," said Mrs. Kramer. "Would you like a drink of juice? Now tell me, what is this all about?"

"Nothing, Mrs. Kramer. I just don't want to be

Nevuchadnezzar any more." Heddy's proud head drooped a little as she stared at the floor.

"Well, of course if you don't want to, you don't have to. But it will probably mean the end of the play. It's scheduled for next week and we don't have enough time to start over with someone new for the main part. I suppose we could have an evening of games and community singing instead. And perhaps you could play the piano. But it does seem like a pity. The entire class is participating in the play, and they'd all lose their parts."

Heddy didn't say a word. She just looked at the floor.

"May I ask why you dislike the part of Nevuchadnezzar so much? I would have thought it would be fun to have the main part."

"Not when it makes everyone think I'm mean and bossy and bad!" Heddy blurted out.

"Why Chedva, what makes you think that?" Mrs. Kramer was very surprised.

"I don't think it; I *know* it! Otherwise, why would they call me 'Hedvuchadnezzar'?"

"Maybe because you do such a good job. It's a compliment to your acting skills. But if it bothers you, you could have told them so. I'm sure they would have stopped."

Heddy suddenly remembered how everyone had gone around calling Rachel "RHG" for "Rachel HAMAN Glick" when she had the part of Haman in the Purim play last year. Rachel thought it was hysterical. She even signed her homework with the middle initial "H" all through the month of Adar.

"You were chosen for the part of Nevuchadnezzar because you can act well, not because you're bad," Mrs. Kramer continued. "If you were an evil person acting the part of a good one, no one would think you were really good. And if you're a good person acting the part of an evil one, no one thinks you are suddenly bad! They only think you're a marvelous actress! Don't take everything so seriously, Heddy. Sometimes we have to learn to laugh a little. Even at ourselves!"

Heddy looked up at kind Mrs. Kramer. Suddenly she felt very silly. "I guess so," she mumbled. "I'm sorry."

"Don't apologize," said Mrs. Kramer. "Just come to school tomorrow and give them a rip-roaring rehearsal with an Evil King they'll remember!"

The play was a huge success and Heddy and her First Assistant Miriam were called back to the stage again and again.

"You were a great First Assistant," said Heddy on their seventh curtain call.

"And you were a great king! I'm getting a crimp in my back from bowing so much," Miriam whispered to Heddy. Heddy giggled.

"I never saw such a smiley evil king," Heddy's

father said later in the evening. "One would think he'd look a little grouchier."

"Nevuchadnezzar *did* look grouchy, I'm sure, Dad," said Heddy. "But I'm not him. I'm me. And I learned something from this play. It pays to remember who you are, and once you remember, it pays to keep smiling! And," she added to herself, "to cooperate."

so much for Snowball

Heddy was up bright and early studying for a math test when she heard Mr. Sendler, the milkman. Mr. Sendler brought them milk straight from his private dairy twice a week, but Heddy hardly ever saw him because he always came so early. This time she hurried to open the kitchen door and say hello.

"Hi, Mr. Sendler! How are your cows?"

"Oh, they're fine, thank you. I have six new calves this year. You should really come see them sometime, Heddy. I have puppies, too."

"You do? Oh, how wonderful! I'd love to have a puppy. You're so lucky!"

"I don't know about that. I don't have a puppy — I have seven! No one seems to want any either, and I don't know what to do with them. You're more than welcome to take one, if you'd like."

"I am? Do you really mean it, Mr. Sendler? I'd *love* to take one!"

"Well, you'd better ask your parents first."

"My mother is still sleeping and my father hasn't

come back from *shul* yet, but I'm sure they won't mind a bit!"

"How do you know?"

"My parents like animals. They told me I could have a pet to keep me company now that my brothers are away at yeshiva and no one is home except me."

"Well...I do have one little feller in my truck. I brought him along on today's route, hoping maybe I'd find a home for him. Would you like to see him?"

Heddy skipped out to Mr. Sendler's truck. She was bursting with curiosity. But when Mr. Sendler brought a tiny handful of white fluff out of a basket in his truck, all she could say was "Oooh!"

"Kinda cute, isn't he?" asked Mr. Sendler smiling. "Sorta like a little snowball."

"That's the *perfect* name for him, Mr. Sendler...Snowball!"

"He's still kinda little. Only a month old. You can have the basket he was in. Keep him warm and feed him milk with breadcrumbs three or four times a day. I'll be back next Tuesday, and if your parents say you can keep him, you'll have to take him to the vet for a checkup and shots. If they don't want him, I'll take him back."

Although Heddy heard Mr. Sendler talking, she wasn't really listening. She was looking at a little, round, squiggly puppy — the smallest, cutest puppy she had ever seen. He was completely covered with soft, white, curly fur. At one end, a tiny white tail wagged furiously; at the other end, a pair of big brown eyes and a shiny black nose peeped through a mass of furry curls. Heddy barely remembered to look up at the kindly milkman and say "Thank you! Thank you so much!"

"Don't thank me yet," he answered. "Let's wait and see if your parents like him."

There was no doubt whatsoever in Heddy's mind that her parents would like him. How could anyone *not* like him? He was the most wonderful animal she had ever seen. Once, when she was six, she had a turtle named Kolonomus, but how could you possibly compare a cold, silent turtle with this absolutely delicious, adorable puppy?

Just then, Dad walked in. "Good morning, Heddy my love! Still studying? What are you holding?"

Mom came cheerfully into the kitchen. "Good morning everyone! Heddy, what is that?"

"It's Snowball! Mr. Sendler brought him. Isn't he gorgeous?"

"What did he bring him *for*?" asked Dad.

"For us, Dad! He needs a home!"

"Who? Mr. Sendler?"

"No!! The puppy!! He has six brothers and sisters and Mr. Sendler can't keep them all. He said to ask your permission and to let him know when he comes back next Tuesday. Isn't he lovely? Of course, I'll take care of him by myself; he won't be any trouble at all. Doesn't he look just like a little snowball?"

Mom took the puppy from Heddy. "He is kind of cute, isn't he?"

"Just a minute," said Dad. "Let's get things straight right now. There will be no dogs in this house. I am not going to *daven* or learn or *bentch* or make *kiddush* with a dog under my feet. I am not going to have a dog barking and disturbing my sleep or the neighbors'. I am not going to babysit for a dog or clean up a dog's mess. This is a people-house, not a dog-house!"

"But Dad, he won't bark. I promise you he won't! Anyone can see how quiet and well behaved he is. Look."

Heddy held the dog out to her father and quick as a wink, the puppy licked Mr. Levi on the nose. "See, he likes you! Oh dad, I just *have* to keep him. You *said* I could have a pet because it's so lonely here without the boys. And he won't be a *single* bit of trouble. I promise he won't!"

"Maybe we can put him in the yard in a dog-house," Mom suggested.

"He's too little! Mr. Sendler said he has to be kept warm. And he'll be afraid out there all by himself. He's used to sleeping with his brothers and sisters."

"So let's send him back there right away before he gets lonesome," said Dad.

"How about the basement?" Mom asked Dad. "Do you think we might keep him in the basement?

At least until Mr. Sendler comes back and we've made our mind up?"

"My mind is already made up," Dad said.

"But you might change it by next week," said Heddy. "You told me that thinking people often change their minds."

"Not about dogs, they don't," he said.

"Well we can't just throw him out!" cried Heddy. "It's *tzaar baal chayim!*"

"Don't worry, dear," said Mom. "We won't abandon him. We'll find him a place, at least until Tuesday. Is the basement all right, or do you want to put him in the garage?"

Heddy looked at Mr. Levi. Her eyes were full of tears. "I suppose the basement will do," he muttered.

Somehow, Heddy not only finished her *Chumash* test that morning in school, but she even finished with her usual mark of One Hundred. The afternoon wore on, but finally, Heddy and Rachel were racing back home — straight to the basement where they spent the rest of the day. In the evening, Mrs. Levi came down.

"Heddy, do you think you can manage to come upstairs to eat dinner and maybe go to sleep tonight? And do not ask if you can sleep with Snowball. The answer is no."

Early the next morning, a heart-wrenching squeal tore through the house, followed by a loud yell which sounded strangely like Heddy's father. Heddy leaped out of bed and ran into her parents' room. Mom was holding Snowball while dad was on his feet, shaking his fist at the little puppy. He was angry.

"I told you this dog was a bad idea. What's he doing on the floor at the edge of my bed? I thought he was put in the basement? I do not expect to step on dogs when I get out of bed! I might have squashed him to death!"

"The dog's not hurt, dear, but are you all right?" Mom asked worriedly.

"I am fine. What I want to know is, how did that dog get up here? Heddy??"

"Um…yeh…uh, good morning Dad. I guess he walked up."

"Through the basement door?"

"Oh…uh…no, I guess not. The door wasn't closed. I left it just a tiny bit open, so I could hear him if he cried. I guess he sort of slipped through and came up. He must really like you if he lay down under *your* bed, Dad. He could have come to me or Mom, couldn't he? "

"He could also have stayed in the basement. Better yet, he could go in the garage. Best of all, he could go back to Mr. Sendler!"

"Heddy," said Mom after Dad left for *shul*, "I really do think the dog should be put in the garage until Mr. Sendler comes for him. This *is* your father's house, not the dog's. I'll fix up a nice basket with an old blanket. It's not cold out now. He'll be fine."

"Just tell me one thing," said Heddy stubbornly. "Don't you think that Dad is being unreasonable and unfair? Don't I have any rights around here? Doesn't anyone care about how *I* feel? Don't I live here too, or am I just a boarder?"

Mrs. Levi smiled. "No, I don't think you're a boarder, dear. Boarders pay rent, and if I'm not mistaken, I think you stay here for free. In addition, I think your father pays for all of your expenses and bills. And I also think that generally speaking, he's a pretty fair fellow.

"I'm not too sure what rights you have or don't have, but you don't seem very underprivileged to me. And we both know that Dad cares about you very much indeed. But he does *not* care for dogs. Even puffy, roly-poly dogs as cute as Snowball. And that is one of *his* rights — not caring for dogs in his own home. So... I think that Snowball will just have to go."

There didn't seem to be much left to say after Mom's speech, so Heddy kept quiet. For three whole days, she didn't say a single word to her father except for "good morning" and "good night". But she did cry, a good deal of the time, so that her eyes were all puffy and red and teary.

But during those three silent days, something

strange was happening in the Levi household. It began when Mom asked Dad to please leave a bowl of milk and breadcrumbs in the garage for Snowball, and Snowball jumped for joy at the sight of Mr. Levi, stepping right into his milkbowl and turning it upside down. Mr. Levi lifted the wet puppy out of the bowl, wiped him off and brought a new bowl of milk in its place.

Then, the next morning, Rachel's mother saw Mr. Levi stopping to pat the puppy on his way out to work.

Then, Aviva's father met Mr. Levi late one night walking the little puppy on a leash. "Since when do you have a dog?" he asked.

"We don't. We're only keeping this one for another day or two. He is kind of cute, though, don't you think?"

"Looks like a perfect girl's dog to me," said Aviva's father. "All curly and white like that. Like a snowball. I bet your daughter really likes him. I wish my Aviva would ask for a dog, but she's scared stiff of anything on four legs."

"Hm..." thought Mr. Levi.

Monday night, Mr. Levi had a talk with Heddy. "Now I don't want you to think I'm just giving in to your Grand Silence and Tears Campaign because I'm not! But as you said I said, thinking people do change their minds, and maybe I was overreacting a bit. Maybe, if we keep him outside, a dog isn't so bad. But we really should teach him how to bark. If we're going to have a dog, he might as well be a watchdog. Although I can't imagine anyone being scared off by a Snowball!"

Heddy was so overjoyed that she didn't know what to do first to show her father how grateful she was. When he began sneezing a few hours later, she rushed to bring him a box of tissues and a glass of tea. "It's nothing," he said, "just the start of a cold."

That evening, he was sneezing every few minutes. All night long he sneezed, wiped his drippy nose, and sneezed again. By the morning he had gone through three boxes of tissues.

"I made an appointment for you with the doctor," said Mrs. Levi. "I've never seen you like this before! Come on, I'll drive." The poor man couldn't even stop sneezing long enough to argue.

Dr. Schwartz examined Mr. Levi carefully. "I can't find a thing wrong with you," he said. "Tell me, do you have something new in the house — a cat? Or a dog?"

"Why, yes," said Mrs. Levi. "A little, furry puppy. He wouldn't hurt a flea."

Dr. Schwartz sat back in his big black chair and laughed. "I'll bet you a gefilte fish that your puppy is the problem. Get rid of him for a few days and see what happens. I'd say your husband is highly allergic to little, furry puppies!"

Heddy couldn't believe it. After her father had finally agreed to the dog! "But he's not even in the house. He's in the garage," she said. "I can sleep there with him and eat there and I won't get near Dad so he won't sneeze."

"Don't be ridiculous, Heddy. Your father is willing to give up a dog, but he's not about to give up his daughter! There's just nothing at all to talk about. I'm really sorry, and so is Dad, but you have to keep your priorities straight." And with that Mrs. Levi went back to cooking dinner.

Heddy went to her room to think about "priorities", but there wasn't really much to think about. She could run away with Snowball, but even as she said it, she knew it was, as Mom said, "ridiculous". So, as usual, she talked it all out with Rachel.

"I mean, I can't give up my Dad, can I? Not that I want to!" she hurried to say. "He's the best dad I ever had. He's smart and kind and fair, and *he* always does the right thing, even when it's hard for him. In fact, I never should have aggravated him so much about a mere dog in the first place!"

Heddy looked at Snowball. He wagged his tail and nestled down in her lap. Her eyes filled up with tears again.

"Mr. Sendler will find him another home," Rachel said. "Don't worry. After all, *kibud av* is tons more important than having a dog! And it's not as if it's your dad's fault. He wasn't allergic on purpose. It's like you and the chocolate. You didn't *want* to be allergic."

"So if I know all these things, why do I feel so bad about giving Snowball back?" asked a sniffy Heddy. "You'd think doing the right thing would make you happy, wouldn't you?"

Rachel sighed in sympathy.

"Well, if we're going to do it, we might as well get it done. I'll get his basket ready and Mr. Sendler will be here in the morning."

Tuesday morning came as expected, and Mr. Sendler came along with it.

"Heddy? I'm so glad you're up on time to meet me. I wanted to talk to you. I've been worrying ever since I was last here. I just hate to be an Indian giver, but I was wondering if you might let me have Snowball back? You see, my grandson Yossi has a birthday tomorrow, but no one bothered to tell me that he set his heart on Snowball for a present. I offered him all the other puppies, but he only wants this one."

"Oh Mr. Sendler," she cried, "you didn't have to worry one bit. You see, my father has this dog allergy and I can't keep Snowball after all!" Heddy was so relieved that she hugged the two bottles of milk she was holding!

"I guess I wasn't supposed to be a permanent dog-owner. Just a temporary dog-keeper, to help me get my priorities straight."

"Beg your pardon?" said Mr. Sendler.

"Never mind," said Heddy happily. "It all worked out fine. Please send my biggest birthday regards to your grandson."

"I will. Oh...I forgot to tell you," Mr. Sendler said on his way out. "You and Yossi must be kindred spirits. Yossi gave the dog a name too, soon as the puppies were born. Do you know what he called him? Snowball, just like you!"

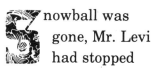

practice makes perfect

nowball was gone, Mr. Levi had stopped sneezing, and now Heddy was looking for something new and interesting to keep herself busy.

"Can't you just relax?" asked her father. "You're busy all day long at school. Isn't that interesting enough? Why do you have to do something interesting at home too?"

"You don't want me to be bored when I come home, do you Dad? We learned in class that it's not good to sit around doing nothing. It gets you into trouble."

"Maybe doing nothing gets *other* people into trouble; *you* seem to get into trouble whenever you're busy doing interesting things!"

"Am I really so bad?" asked Heddy worriedly.

"Of course you're not!" answered Mrs. Levi quickly. "You know your father is just teasing you. You're actually a very lovely young lady and we're very proud of you — the way you took care of the Twins, the way you gave up Snowball. In fact, the way you do most things!"

"In that case," said Heddy, "I'm going to try and give you something else to be proud of. I decided to sew a dress."

"Go right ahead. As long as I don't have to help," said Mr. Levi.

"Hm...are you sure that isn't too complicated a project?" asked Mrs. Levi. "You haven't had any real sewing lessons, just my instructions for fixing hems. Why don't you start with something easier, like an apron?"

"A dish-washing apron," Mr. Levi suggested hopefully.

"I never wear aprons. Besides, Aviva has a wonderful super-simple pattern she's giving me. She says absolutely anyone can use it without the slightest trouble. It'll be a whizz. All I need is money to buy material."

"Can't you take one of your old dresses apart and use the material? Then, if the new dress doesn't come out so 'whizzy' at least you won't have wasted any money." Mr. Levi was always so practical.

"That's impossible, Dad. What if the old dress was cut differently? All I need is five dollars. That's not too much, is it? A new dress from the store would cost lots more. Just think — this might be the beginning of a real career. Do you know how much money I could save on clothes for Mom and me?"

Mr. Levi shrugged his shoulders. "Well, we'll

hope for the best." He handed Heddy a five dollar bill. "Good luck."

Heddy was soon on her way to the fabric store with Aviva. "I don't know why my father isn't more optimistic," she said. "He always seems to expect the worst. Especially when it has to do with me."

"Don't worry," Aviva consoled her. "When he sees the gorgeous Shabbos dress you'll have made, he'll beg you to sew some more!"

On that happy note, the two girls went into the store and emerged twenty minutes later with a large bag.

"I just don't understand it, Heddy! You got the zipper in upside down. The two sides don't match either. One is higher than the other. And the sleeves look funny. I think you put the right one in backwards."

"I *couldn't* have!" Heddy insisted. "I followed the instructions perfectly! I didn't change a thing!"

"Maybe we'd better show it your mother," said Aviva. "I can't figure out what you did to it. All I know is, it doesn't look like a dress is supposed to look."

Mrs. Levi shook her head sadly. "I don't think I can do anything to straighten it out either. Why didn't you ask me to help before you cut the material, Heddy?"

"Because it all looked so easy. And Aviva said it

was super-simple. Even her younger sister sewed one all by herself."

"Well, it's not a complete waste. We can take it apart and sew up a few aprons. And it's good material for rags. I can always use rags."

"Five dollar rags?" muttered Mr. Levi from the other room.

"Or we could use it for Purim," said Aviva. "It would make a wonderful costume!"

"It would?" asked Heddy doubtfully. "What kind?"

"A clown!" answered Aviva enthusiastically.

Heddy sighed. "I guess I won't be a dressmaker after all. I don't have enough sewing patience. It's even easier to be patient with the Twins than with zippers and sleeves!"

The dress was put away and forgotten, and Heddy had a new idea instead.

"I'll bake! That's what! I know something about baking. I've watched Mom a million times and I know exactly how to go about it, even without a pattern. Baking is *really* super-simple."

Heddy invited Rachel to come over Wednesday afternoon during their lunch hour. But instead of eating, they sifted and measured and poured and mixed and made a magnificent batch of banana batter, enough for a triple layer cake.

"Stop eating it, Rachel! There won't be anything left!"

"It's really good, Heddy," said Rachel. "It's going to be a wonderful cake — high, light and fluffy. Will you save me a slice?"

"Of course I will! And Rachel, do you know what? *Shabbos* is my father's birthday! I'm going to make this a birthday cake for him! Then he'll see that I don't always get into trouble when I'm busy!"

They poured the batter carefully into three layer pans and put them gently into the warm oven. Then they sat down to wait.

"Maybe we should start cleaning up while we're waiting for it to bake," Rachel suggested.

"I'm afraid to," Heddy answered. "I want to concentrate on the waiting. Otherwise we'll forget to take the cake out of the oven before we go to school and it will burn!"

Rachel shook her head. "I don't think your mother will appreciate coming home to such a messy kitchen. I'll clean up while you concentrate." So Rachel cleaned and Heddy concentrated. And they both waited. The clock on the wall ticked the minutes away until it was time to return to school, but still the cake wasn't ready.

"What should we do?" Rachel asked. "I don't want to be late for class."

"We'll just have to take the cake out of the oven and finish baking it when school is over," said the practical Heddy.

"Are you sure that's the right thing to do? I never

saw my mother take a half-finished cake out of the oven."

"I'm not sure, but I hope so. We have to go back to school, and we can't leave it in or it will burn. So out it goes!"

Heddy removed the three pans and put them on the counter.

At four fifteen, the girls rushed back from school and found the cakes exactly where they had left them.

"They look a little lower, don't you think?" asked Rachel.

"Sort of. I guess they fell in. But I'm sure they'll rise again once the oven starts warming them up."

The cakes went back in; the girls sat and waited. Half an hour later, Heddy decided that they had baked enough. She opened the oven and coughed as a puff of smoke wafted out.

"Oy! They're burnt!" cried Heddy.

"No they aren't! They're just very slightly browned! A little banana frosting will cover it up. But look, Heddy, they don't seem to have risen any, do they?"

And they did not. They were low and leathery. Like three sturdy, flat, rubbery wheels.

"So what? I'm sure they'll taste fine. Didn't you hear Mrs. Kramer say the other day: Don't look at the outside of a vessel; look inside it."

"These aren't vessels; they're cakes," thought

Rachel. But all she said was, "Well, it's a good thing you made three layers and not just two. Three low layers are just like two high ones."

Just then, Heddy dropped the second layer. "Be careful! You'll break it!" cried Rachel. But it didn't break at all. It just bounced. Three times. Like a ball.

"Oy Rachel! It bounces! Cakes aren't supposed to bounce!"

Rachel — good, patient, optimistic Rachel — hurried to say, "You're lucky it bounced! The bouncing stopped it from breaking!"

So Heddy frosted her bouncy-banana cake and by the time she was finished, it looked ready to be eaten — just like any other normal, respectable, cheerful birthday cake.

Shabbat came. The family ate and sang *zemirot*. Then it was time for dessert. Instead of their regular chocolate mousse or fruit compote, Heddy brought out her lovely cake accompanied by a hearty "Happy Birthday" greeting. Mr. Levi found it a little hard to cut so he asked for a sharper knife. After a few sawing motions, he got into the swing of things and cut a large piece for Heddy.

"Maybe you'd better cut smaller pieces until we see how it tastes," suggested Heddy.

"Absolutely not!" insisted her father. "I'm sure it's delicious! I'm going to have a double-size-slice of the first birthday cake my daughter ever baked me!"

With that, he cut himself a double portion and began to chew. And chew. And chew. After the first few bites, Mrs. Levi very politely put her fork down. "I'm really too full to eat so much cake now," she said. "I'll finish it later."

After a few more bites, Heddy also gave up. "It's like eating frosted rubber." But Mr. Levi perservered.

"Don't you think that's enough, dear?" asked Mrs. Levi.

"You do as you like," he said, "but I think this cake is delicious, and I intend to finish every crumb on my plate."

Piece after piece, he sawed and cut and chewed as Heddy and her mother silently watched. When he finally finished, he said the *birkat hamazon* quickly and went to lie down.

"I don't think my cake was such a great success, Mom," said Heddy as they cleaned off the table. "Maybe I'd better stick to schoolwork and leave the baking to you."

"Don't be silly," said her mother. "You just need a little practice to succeed. You know what they say, 'Practice makes perfect.'"

"In sewing too?"

"In everything."

Heddy sighed. If there was anything she hated, it was practicing. She liked things to get done quickly and easily; more or less by themselves. However, if practicing was what was needed to succeed in life, practice she would. Tomorrow was a new week. She would start first thing in the morning.

a happy medium

What is going on in this house?" Mr. Levi's voice could be heard loud and strong, even over the scales Heddy was playing on the piano.

"What's wrong, Dad?" she called.

"Why are you making so much noise?"

"I'm not making noise. I'm practicing!"

"Why are you practicing at six-thirty on a Sunday morning? You'll wake up the entire neighborhood!"

"I closed the windows. I just wanted to get a head start. I have a concert in two weeks, and I have to practice in order to do a good job. Practice makes perfect. That's what Mom says. Even though I'm scared I'll fail, if I practice, *b'ezrat Hashem*, I'll succeed. So I'm practicing."

Mr. Levi groaned. "Heddy…dearest, darling Heddy…I beg of you…please, please don't practice for your concert before the sun comes up! Your poor old father is allergic to music when he's sleeping."

"But isn't it time for you to go to *minyan*?" Heddy asked.

"I didn't sleep too well last night; I had some stomach cramps. So I wasn't intending to go to the early *minyan* this morning. I can still sleep for another half an hour if the early-morning-music stops."

Heddy drooped. "Gee, I can't even practice successfully. Maybe I have to practice how to practice in order to succeed. Oh well, I'll *daven* and eat breakfast first and practice afterwards. I suppose it doesn't make any difference."

Heddy returned to the piano an hour later and began again. Every so often, Mrs. Levi came into the room to offer some musical advice.

At nine-thirty, Aviva called. "Meet you outside in half an hour," she announced.

"Sorry. I'm busy practicing for my concert."

At ten-thirty, Rachel called. "Do you want to go to the Old Age Home with us this morning?"

"Sorry. Not today. I'm busy practicing piano."

At twelve, Miriam came over. "We're going swimming. You coming?"

"Next week. I have to practice now."

At one o'clock, Mr. Levi came in and said, "Heddy, don't you want to stop? That's plenty for one morning. There are thirteen more days until the concert. You don't have to get all your practicing done today. Leave a little for tomorrow!"

The next two weeks, Heddy continued to practice. In the morning before school and in the afternoon when she came home. She practiced in the evening too. She learned all the music by heart, and her fingers even moved in her sleep!

"It's good, Heddy," said her mother. "It really is. My students at the music conservatory don't do half as well. Your teacher will be proud of you." And still Heddy practiced some more.

Finally, thirteen days later, she found herself in front of a shiny grand piano in a large hall filled with people, all sitting politely, waiting for her to begin. She felt as though a nest of hornets was churning round and round in her stomach.

"Relax, Heddy! You know this piece backwards and forwards!" Mrs. Levi whispered from the back of the stage.

There was no use waiting any longer. It was now or never. Heddy began. She didn't even think about the music. All she knew was that her hands were trembling and she was afraid they would hit the wrong notes. But she didn't have to worry. Her hands went about their musical business automatically, without the tiniest mistake. They hadn't been practicing faithfully, night and day, for several weeks, for nothing!

Heddy finished to loud applause. When she got up to take a bow, she discovered that her hands were fine, but now her knees were shaking!

Her teacher came up to the stage with a big smile. "That was a *wonderful* musical rendition, and instead of the normal, expected encore, I am pleased to announce a surprise. As you all know, Heddy's mother is one of the teachers at the conservatory, and she tells me that she and Heddy will now play a duet for us."

A duet?! Heddy gasped. What had Mom done? What duet? They hadn't practiced, or even discussed, playing for the concert! Mrs. Levi walked up to the stage and sat down on the bench next to Heddy.

"Relax!" she whispered. "We're going to be great!"

"But what are we going to play???" Heddy's stomach was churning again.

"Our Hebrew music and the *zemirot Shabbat*. The same way we play every *Motzai Shabbat* for the family. Ready? Let's go!"

Heddy hardly had a minute to think before Mrs. Levi began playing. "Oh well," she thought, "here goes!" and she started too. But this time, she didn't have to think or worry one bit. Her hands and knees behaved beautifully and Heddy and her mother ended to the sound of loud clapping and enthusiastic cries of "Encore! Encore!"

"Gee," said a thoroughly surprised Heddy, "we were great!"

"You sure were," agreed Mr. Levi. "Even better than The Klezmerim — that band that Jeremy and Sammy organized when they were in seventh

grade, remember? I was their conductor."

"And I didn't even practice for the duet. Why did it turn out so well?"

"Because you relaxed and did your best," said Mr. Levi. "That's always a good way to do things."

"I'll have to remember that," thought Heddy. "Relax and do your best."

The next week at school, Mrs. Kramer returned the *dinim* tests to the girls. Heddy stuck hers into her schoolbag without even looking at it. She expected her usual One Hundred. At the very worst, maybe a Ninety Five.

"Chedva," said Mrs. Kramer after class, "don't you want to discuss your test with me?"

"My test? What for?"

"Well, it isn't exactly your usual grade."

"It isn't? I didn't look." Heddy pulled the wrinkled paper out of her bag and couldn't believe her eyes. It was marked Forty Seven!

"Did you make a mistake, Mrs. Kramer?" she asked.

"No. But I think *you* made a few! What happened? Didn't you study?"

"Well…sort of…but not exactly. That is, I always learn everything pretty quickly in school. Then I review it at home, just to make sure. This time, I decided not to bother with reviewing. I just relaxed and did my best! Like my Dad told me to."

Mrs. Kramer didn't know whether to smile or to sigh. "Chedva," she said, "you always seem to go full speed ahead — if not in one direction, then in another. When it's Practice-Makes-Perfect, you practice perfection until you collapse. And when it's Relax-and-Do-Your-Best, you relax so well that you barely remember the time of day! Can't you aim for a happy medium?"

"How?" asked poor Heddy. "Should I try less and relax more? Or relax less and try more?"

"A happy medium is somewhere in the middle."

"You mean, somewhere between Complete Perfection and Perfect Relaxation?"

"That's right! Let's call it Relaxed Perfection. You don't have to be at the very top of the ladder all the time. But don't allow yourself to tumble down to the very bottom either!"

Heddy sighed. "Thanks for worrying about me, Mrs. Kramer. I'm sorry I give you so much trouble. But don't worry *too* much."

Heddy suddenly smiled. "You know — aim for a happy medium!"

"I don't know," mumbled Mrs. Kramer as Heddy left the room, "there are just some things they didn't teach us how to deal with in Teachers' College, and Heddy Levi is certainly one of them!"

from rags to riches

Mrs. Levi was practicing a waltz by Chopin on the piano. Heddy was sitting on the couch listening. And talking.

"But Mom, I really do need the raise. My allowance is too small. All the girls get more than I do. All I'm asking for is three dollars more a week."

Mrs. Levi stopped playing and turned to her daughter.

"Heddy, allowances and Chopin don't go together. I really haven't got the strength to argue with you anymore. If you're so insistent, go and ask your father."

"I wasn't trying to argue," said Heddy. "I was trying to discuss. You told me that when people disagree, they should try to discuss things!"

"Twenty minute's worth of discussing is enough for me. Go ask your father."

Mrs. Levi went back to Chopin and Heddy went looking for her father. She found him in the study, his head hidden behind a big pile of *sefarim*. She knew he didn't like to be bothered when he was studying, but she stood quietly in the doorway, hoping he'd look up. He did.

"Yes, Heddy? Did you want something?"

"Yes, please. Three dollars more a week."

"This minute?"

"It's urgent! You see, the girls are going to buy a birthday present for Aviva now and I don't have any money for my part of the gift."

"Where's your allowance money?"

"I lost part of it on Sunday. Besides, it's not enough, Dad. Really. It never lasts past Thursday, the latest. And everyone gets more than I do. Can't I have a raise?"

Mr. Levi sat back in his chair. "Listen Heddy. We went through all this a few months ago. We figured out your expenses very carefully and added a fair sum to be spent or saved, as you wished. You have to learn to be more responsible with your money. It doesn't grow on trees, you know. *My* boss doesn't give me a raise every time I run short of funds, and I don't think I'm going to give you one either. We'll discuss a raise in allowance at the beginning of the next school year. Until then, learn how to budget. Practice a little thrift."

"Could I at least have an advance for Aviva's gift?"

"No advances. It's only Tuesday."

"Then what will I do about Aviva's birthday?"

"I don't know. Give her one of the gifts you

received on *your* birthday. You had a pile of lovely gifts you didn't know what to do with. Is that all?"

Heddy turned and left the study. She was angry. Dad wasn't being fair. She *did* budget and she *was* responsible but her money disappeared anyway. And it wasn't her fault if she lost the three dollars for Aviva's present. It could have happened to anybody! Terry still owed her a dollar fifty from last month, but she didn't have the money to pay it back yet, so that didn't help any.

"I'll make my own money, that's what I'll do! Then Dad won't have to give me any. I'll show him how responsible I can be! Jeremy and Sammy did it once when they opened their employment agency, and I can do it too! I'm going to call Rachel and ask if she wants to help me right now."

"But what can we make money with?" Rachel wanted to know. "I'm willing to help, but I have to know what we're doing!"

"Dad said I should be thrifty, so I decided to open a thrift shop. People always have things to give away. They can give them to us and we'll sell them to other people who want them."

"What if nobody wants them?"

"Someone will. You'll see. I'll ask if we can use our garage. I'm sure Dad won't mind as long as we keep things clean. And Terry's mom has a package of used baby clothing to give away. It can be our first donation! "

"We'll need more merchandise than that," said Rachel. "Let's put some signs up around the neighborhood before we open. I think my aunt has an old crib and playpen she wants to get rid of."

One thing led to another, and within a week, the Levi's garage was full. The shelves on one wall were neatly stacked with *Children's Clothing*; one wall held *Toys and Books*; one was for *Adult Clothing*; and one was for *Miscellaneous and Household Items*. Everything was clean and in good condition, with lists of prices for all items in each department.

Sunday afternoon found Heddy and Rachel swamped with buyers. They cleared out all the stock. But on Monday, new merchandise started coming in — a used toy truck, an old typewriter, a set of encyclopedia from the year 1979, thirty-two balls of pink wool, twenty-five coloring books, a beautiful cuckoo clock which didn't cuckoo. Mr. Sendler's gave them three puppies — Snowball's sisters — which they took on the condition that if no one bought them by the end of the day, he would take them back to the milk farm.

But the most exciting contribution was from Terry's uncle David. He asked them if they wanted his old run-down car. After seventeen years, he finally bought a new one and he was willing to give the old one to anyone who would tow it away from his house. The towing would cost fifteen dollars.

"That's half our profit for the week," said Rachel.

"I don't think we should take the car."

"But Rachel, you have to invest in order to earn. Remember the family who used to live down the street? Their son Yossi was a friend of my brother Danny. He said he'll pay us twenty five dollars for the car. So if we bring it here, we'll have earned ten dollars! The only problem is that Yossi only has fifteen dollars now, so we'd have to keep the car for three weeks until he saves the other ten."

"Heddy Levi, I warn you! Your father won't like that wreck sitting in front of your house for three weeks."

"I know. But it's a pity to lose that ten dollars."

"Then tell Yossi to tow the car to *his* house and to pay the garage the fifteen dollar towing fee. He can pay us the other ten when he has the money. It's called 'extending credit'. All businesses do it."

"Rachel, you are a financial *genius*! Why didn't I think of that?"

The next item Heddy and Rachel found in their garage was an old dining room set. There were no buyers.

"My father says we have to get rid of it by tomorrow afternoon."

"So why did you take it, Heddy? You know it's too big for us to handle."

"But an entire dining room set, Rachel! Think of what it's worth!"

"My father always says a thing is only worth

what you can get for it, and if no one wants it, it's not worth anything!"

But this time, Mrs. Levi came to the rescue. "I've found you an owner, girls."

"You mean a buyer, Mom."

"Nope. I mean an owner. They aren't buying, but they'll take it off your hands. The Old Age Home can use your dining room set and they'll send a pickup truck to collect it. It's just what the doctor ordered! Be glad."

"That's great, Mom. It really is. It can sort of be a *tzedaka* donation. In fact, they might be able to use a big package of magazines we received. We were going to charge ten cents apiece for them, but we'd be happy to give them to the Old Age Home, wouldn't we Rachel?"

"Sure. And we'll throw in the bag of cassettes with all the songs and music that came in today too."

Then came something bigger yet. Bigger than the car, and bigger than the dining room set. At that point, Mr. Levi put his foot down.

"NO! You cannot take an expensive, twenty foot, free standing, concrete swimming pool, even if the Bergers are willing to take it apart and deliver it! Not even if it doesn't leak! No, not even if it's for free! I have no intention of parking my car in a swimming pool in the garage!"

But even that problem solved itself. Heddy and

Rachel sold the pool at a big discount to the Children's Hospital. Volunteers came to pick it up, and they left a check for one hundred dollars, made out to Heddy and Rachel.

"Wow! One hundred dollars! And all we did was make a few phone calls! How can Dad say I'm not thrifty or responsible?"

But the last surprise was the best of all. It was *really* big; even bigger than the pool. And it was absolutely unmoveable. It was a house. A very small, old house, it's true, but a house nonetheless. With a garden, a tree, and a fence. It stood at the far end of town, near the tire factory. It belonged to old Mrs. Shriver who was trying to sell it for years. When she heard about the thrift shop and all of the contributions Heddy and Rachel were making to worthy causes, she decided to donate the house and garden to them, to use as they wished.

"Your father has helped me many times in the past, Heddy," she said. "Now that I'm going to live with my son in California, I don't need the house anymore. I've tried to sell it, but no one wants to live near the tire factory, and I can't afford the taxes anymore. So you take it as a thank you to your father for all the favors he's done for me." And she had her lawyers transfer the property to Mr. Gershon Levi, Miss Chedva Levi, and Miss Rachel Travis.

"It's half yours, Dad," said Heddy. "Mrs. Shriver gave it to us because of you."

Mr. Levi, however, wasn't very appreciative. "If anyone had asked me, I would have given it right back! What in heaven's name will we do with it except pay more taxes on the property? Maybe Rachel's father wants it? No? Well, you two are the business tycoons here. Find a way to get rid of it!"

But this time they were stumped. You'd think that someone would want a free house and garden, even if they were near the tire factory. But no one did. Not a single person. Finally, Mr. Levi stepped in.

"Okay," he said. "I talked to my *shul* committee. The *shul* is pretty crowded and we need some more room for all of our activities. Maybe we can use the house as an activity center and study center. I'll contact my lawyer and we'll see if we can convince the city to rezone the property. But on one condition. No more business. You close the thrift shop and empty out the garage so I can park my car in there again."

Here Mr. Levi stopped for a moment and took a deep breath. "And I," he continued, "will raise your allowance by three dollars a week so that you can stay solvent."

talk, talk, talk

The Levi's were eating dinner. Actually, Mr. and Mrs. Levi were eating. Heddy was talking. About Mrs. Kramer and the wonderful way she explained things in class; about the sour milk in the lunchroom; about Terry's new baby brother; about the broken traffic light opposite the shopping center; about...well, just about everything and anything she saw or heard or said or thought of.

"Heddy dear, your soup is getting cold. You'll tell us the end of the story after dinner. Start eating now."

"In a minute, Mom. Did you know that Aviva sewed a new dress for her sister? It's two pieces, with green pockets and straps like this over the shoulders and..."

"And eat your soup already!" said Mr. Levi.

"I didn't finish describing the dress. Besides, I don't want the soup. It's cold. Oh, I almost forgot. Did I tell you about my math test yesterday?" And on it went.

Finally, Mr. Levi spoke up. "Heddy, *Hashem* gave ten measures of speech to the world. If you use them all up, there won't be any left for anyone else!"

"Oh Dad, I don't talk *that* much."

"I don't know how much is 'that much', but if you don't stop talking and start eating, you're going to starve to death!"

"I'll eat, I promise. It's just that I have so many things to tell you first!"

"They'll wait until after the soup. Meanwhile, your mother and I would like a chance to talk to each other too!"

"Who's stopping you from talking?"

"No one at all! It's just hard to get a word in edgewise around here!"

Heddy was insulted. Here she was, telling her parents all of the important things that happened to her that day, and they obviously weren't very interested. All they could think of was the things *they* wanted to say! Very well; she'd be quiet. She wouldn't say a word. She'd eat her dinner in utter silence.

Mom and Dad began their own conversation. They hardly seemed to notice that Heddy wasn't participating. They asked her a question or two and continued talking. Heddy thought their conversation was very dull. Hers had been much more interesting.

That night, before she went to sleep, Heddy asked

her mother, "Mom, do you really think I talk too much?"

"Heddy," she said, "you are a very observant, lively and interesting girl. But that doesn't mean you have to share every single thought that passes through your head with the people around you. Give other people a chance to say what they're thinking and feeling. You want others to listen to you, don't you? Then you have to listen to them once in a while too. Besides, it's good to give your vocal chords a rest!"

The next day, all day long, Heddy thought about talking. And about not talking. Or at least about not talking so much. Perhaps Mom was right. She *did* have a lot to say, and she usually said it. Maybe she should say less and give everyone else a chance to say more. She decided she'd try it for a few days and see what happened.

The first person she met in the afternoon was Edna. Edna learned in a school in the next township, so she didn't see Heddy very often. But when she did, she had lots of things to talk about. And talk she did.

She told Heddy about her family, her school, her friends; her brother's wedding, the bride's dress, the *sheva brachot*; the sales in the shopping center, the new wallpaper in her bedroom, and her braces. Heddy listened and didn't say a word. After half an hour of listening, she looked at her watch and cried,

"Oh Edna, I'm so late! I had a doctor's appointment ten minutes ago!" and she ran for her life. As she was running, Edna called after her, "It's always great to see you, Heddy. We have such good conversations together!"

Heddy's head was reeling. She hurried home and lay down to rest. When her mother came into the house, she rushed downstairs.

"Oh Mom, I met Edna and it was dreadful! I even told a lie, just to get away from her. I said I had to go to the doctor. Do you think it's as bad as a regular lie? I didn't mean to lie, but it was the only thing I could think of that wouldn't insult her and I just *had* to get away!"

"I'm glad you didn't insult her, Heddy. Of course you could have said you had to leave, without inventing a doctor's appointment. That would have been sufficient. But sometimes it's hard to think of the right thing at the right time. But why did you have to get away from Edna? Was something wrong?"

Heddy looked uncomfortable.

"I know I shouldn't say this, Mom, but you should hear her! She talked non-stop for half an hour. Really non-stop! I hardly said a single word. My head was pounding by the time she was through."

"I'm sure she didn't mean to monopolize the conversation. Sometimes people don't realize how much they're talking."

"It was so *boring* listening to her go on and on and on."

"I'm sure she thought her conversation was interesting. She was just being friendly and sharing her thoughts with you."

"I don't need so much sharing, thank you. Do I sound like Edna, Mom?"

"You sound like you're verging on a little *lashon hara*."

Heddy looked despairing. "I know," she mumbled.

Mrs. Levi gave her daughter a quick hug. "A little less talk from everyone might not be such a bad idea. *Chazal* teach us that silence is a precious thing; sometimes even more precious than the gift of speech."

Suddenly, Heddy laughed.

"What's so funny?" asked Mrs. Levi.

"It's my turn to give a speech at the *Rosh Chodesh* assembly next week and I didn't know what to talk about. I think I'll talk about — keeping quiet!"

Tamara Sereno

he phone didn't stop ringing. This time it was Terry.

"Did you meet them yet, Heddy? No? How come? They moved in yesterday, didn't they? And they're right next door to you! What's the new girl's name? Isn't she beautiful? Did you see her haircut? And her sandals? And those bracelets? Do you think they're real gold? And the furniture they brought in — wow! It's really something! Call me back as soon as you meet her, OK? Find out if she'll be going to Kerem HaTorah! Don't forget!"

But Heddy didn't go over. Not just yet. Mom and Dad had gone to welcome the Serenos, but not Heddy. Mom had even asked her once or twice if she didn't want to go over too, but Heddy wasn't ready yet.

She didn't know why she was hesitating. She was surely curious enough. But she found herself not liking the new girl, even before she knew her name. She didn't dress like Heddy or her friends. She didn't sound like them either. Heddy heard her calling one of her younger brothers and she had a funny accent, as if she were trying to make herself sound important. Even the family's name — Sereno — was unusual.

But she was beautiful. She really was. Heddy looked in the mirror. "Am I pretty?" she wondered. She had never thought about it very much before. She had a small nose, like Mom, and freckles like Dad, and curly brown hair like Zeidy used to have when he was young. Dad always said she was gorgeous, but he would have said that even if she had crossed eyes and buck teeth.

Heddy wondered if the new girl was smart. It wouldn't be fair if she were beautiful and rich *and* smart. She probably thought she was something really special — with her shiny straight hair and her gold bracelets and all that fancy furniture in her house.

Just then, the new family piled into their big, shiny station wagon and drove away. Heddy sighed. "Well, I'll go over and meet her tomorrow. But I hope she'll go to the other day school. I don't think she'll fit in Kerem HaTorah at all."

The following morning, Heddy woke up ten minutes late and arrived at school after class had started. As she slipped silently into her seat, Mrs. Kramer was introducing Tamara Sereno to the class.

"Tamara's family is originally from Turkey, but

they moved to England ten years ago, and that's where Tamara lived until now. We're delighted to have you in our class, Tamara, and I'm sure the girls will all make you feel at home.

"Sunday is *Rosh Chodesh*, and instead of having our *Rosh Chodesh* get-together at my house as planned, Tamara has very graciously invited the class to a barbecue in her yard at five-thirty. Fortunately, it's right next door to the Levis, so Chedva should manage to get there on time, even if she does have a little trouble making it to class before the bell!"

The girls all laughed good naturedly. Heddy managed a weak grin and slunk down into her seat.

Heddy was glad when they started the weekly *dikduk* lesson. Hebrew grammar was her favorite subject and she was the class star, but not this time. This time, Tamara was the one who knew all the rules, could conjugate all the verbs, could translate all the hard words. Heddy couldn't keep up with her.

Things were no better in math. Tamara was a walking calculator. In science and history she was an encyclopedia. In *Chumash* she was almost as good as Mrs. Kramer, and in *dinim*, she might have been a *rav*!

At one point, Rachel passed her a note which read: You're lucky! You can walk Tamara home from school!

The morning dragged on. When the bell finally

rang for recess, Tamara was surrounded by an admiring audience. Everyone was so busy asking her questions, looking at the pictures in her wallet, and ooh-ing and aah-ing over her clothes, that had Heddy been on the moon, no one would have missed her. Not even Rachel. The minute school was over, Heddy hurried out of the building. Tamara could find her own way home.

The rest of the week was no better, and when Sunday came, Heddy decided: She was *not* going to the barbecue.

"Why not?" asked Mrs. Levi.

"My head hurts."

"Do you have fever?"

"What's the difference? Even if I don't, my head still hurts, and if I go to a smoky barbecue, it'll hurt more. Besides, no one will miss me."

Mrs. Levi sat down. "Heddy, don't you want to tell me what's wrong? You've been miserable all week long, haven't you? Ever since the Serenos moved in."

"Oh Mom, I wish they had never come! I wish they would have moved somewhere else! There are so many places they could have gone...why did they have to come here?"

"Did you have a fight with Tamara?"

"A fight? I haven't even said three words to her!"

"Then what's the matter?"

"I don't like her! That's what! She thinks she's so

rich and smart and beautiful and everyone else thinks so too — except me! I don't understand how the girls can all make such a fuss about her, as if she were someone really special. If she weren't so rich and smart and pretty, she wouldn't be any better than anyone else!"

"Chedva Levi! I can't believe it! Are you jealous?"

"I'm *not* jealous! I'm just annoyed. I don't like stuck-up people!"

Mrs. Levi moved over and made room for her sulky daughter on the sofa. She put her arm around Heddy's shoulder and gave her a squeeze.

"Poor Heddy! No wonder your head hurts! It's a wonder your heart doesn't hurt as well! But there's no medicine for your kind of ache.

"*Chazal* teach us that jealousy is so terrible that it brings its own punishment. It makes us miserable and unhappy and can even shorten our lives! Now why would a bright young lady like you want to make herself miserable for no reason at all?"

Heddy didn't answer.

"First of all, Tamara *is* rich and smart and lovely. These are gifts *Hashem* has given her and she uses them well. She studies and learns and helps the other girls learn too. She seems to share whatever she has, so you can't say she's selfish or stingy. And she *is* lovely.

"But you're lovely too! And so are a lot of your friends. So what if Tamara is a little lovelier? Why can't you just take pleasure in her and enjoy her like the other girls are doing? Do you think that you're less smart or lovely or likeable just because Tamara came? Did Rachel stop being your 'first best friend'? Do Aviva or Miriam or Terry like you less?"

"Oh Mom, I know it's wrong and stupid, but I can't help it. Before Tamara came, even if I was the youngest, at least I was the smartest one in the class. Now no one pays any attention to me and I feel perfectly awful!"

"If *Hashem* has arranged for Tamara to get all that love and attention, there must be a good reason for it. Why don't you just relax and count your own blessings? Be grateful for what you have and be generous with your friends. Whatever you share with them will be returned sevenfold."

"That's very easy for *you* to say. *You* don't have Tamara Sereno in your class!"

Monday afternoon after school Heddy ran into the house, slammed the door, tossed her books on the table and threw herself into her mothers arms. "Oh Mom, it's *so* awful! *I'm* so awful! *Everything* is so awful!"

"What's so awful now Heddy? More Tamara-trouble?"

"Yes, but not what you think! Oh Mom, I'm so ashamed I could just die!" Heddy sobbed away for all she was worth, stopping only to gasp for breath here and there. Mrs. Levi stroked her hair and waited for her to calm down.

"It's Tamara, Mom. She wasn't in school today and Mrs. Kramer said she won't be coming for at least a month or two. She's *sick*! Not just a cold or a sore throat or mumps or something simple like that. She's *really* sick. Something serious. That's why her parents moved here from England. The doctors there couldn't take care of her. She needs some sort of complicated operation. And she didn't even tell anybody. She just smiled all the time and acted as though everything was fine."

"Then how did you find out?"

"Mrs. Kramer told the class today. That's why Tamara wanted to make the barbecue in her yard yesterday. And I didn't go! I stayed home to spite her! I spent the whole time in bed not liking her and feeling sorry for myself because she was so lucky! Oh Mom, I'm so ashamed. And poor Tamara! She must be so scared."

Mrs. Levi sighed. "Poor Tamara indeed," she whispered. "And her poor parents. Well, we'll have a good reason to say *Tehillim* this month, won't we, Heddy? And a good chance to practice some neighborly *gemillat chesed* by pitching in and helping the Serenos out. You can make up your lack of friendliness with an extra measure of *bikkur cholim* — once Tamara is well enough for you to visit, of course."

"Oh, I will, really I will, Mom. But do you think she'll be alright? Mrs. Kramer sounded so solemn and serious when she told us."

"I don't know what's wrong with Tamara, but she's young and there are wonderful doctors here, and between their help and the prayers of all her friends, let's hope that, *b'ezrat Hashem*, Tamara will be well and fine."

Heddy lay awake for a long time in bed that night. Her mind was full of thoughts about jealousy and anger and shame; about fear and worrry; about counting one's blessings and sharing and receiving sevenfold in return. And over and over again, she prayed that Tamara Sereno would have a *refuah shleyma*.

babies and Bat Mitzvas

The girls had just come back from Miriam's house. They had all gone to see her new sister.

"What a delicious baby," sighed Terry. "I just love babies, don't you? She's so tiny and perfect. She even has curly eyelashes!"

"She's beautiful," agreed Heddy, "but she sure takes up a lot of time. Miriam's mother changed her twice and fed her once, all within two and a half hours! It seems pretty tiring. I wonder where she finds the time."

Terry laughed. "You're so funny sometimes, Heddy! That's what parents are for! They're the ones who find the time to take care of babies. Your mother fed and changed you too! Besides," she continued, "when you love a baby, you don't mind doing all that work, even if it does make you tired. Babies even make you tired *before* they're born. They're a full-time job." Terry knew all about babies. She had four younger brothers in her house.

"Heddy hasn't had much baby experience,"

explained Rachel, another eighth-grade baby-expert.

Heddy thought about babies on the way home, but since there didn't seem to be much she could do about them one way or the other, the subject was soon forgotten. After her piano lesson, she had promised Mom she'd help clean the basement and *that* was a *real* job!

Mom was dusting the top shelves of a bookcase while Heddy was sorting her old Olomeinu magazines. Heddy looked at her mother for a moment and then said, "Mom, you've gained weight. You should go on a diet for a week or two." Mrs. Levi just smiled.

Heddy didn't understand what was so amusing about gaining weight, especially since her mother was so careful about what she ate. She always claimed it wasn't healthy to be more than two pounds overweight (although Heddy suspected she was as concerned about the way she looked as about the way she felt!).

Then Mrs. Levi looked at her watch and said, "That's it for now. We'll finish clearing up this mess tomorrow afternoon."

"Tomorrow afternoon?" Heddy looked up from her magazines. "I have to study with Rachel tomorrow afternoon. Why not finish now? We barely started an hour ago."

"I'm tired," said Mrs. Levi. "You can continue working if you like, but I'm through for the day."

Heddy was confused. Mom tired? Mom was *never* tired. And after an hour's work? "You really should think about a diet, Mom," she said. "Maybe those extra pounds are weighing you down."

This time Mrs. Levi laughed out loud. "Maybe they are! But for such a smart daughter, you are sometimes very unobservant! Haven't you noticed anything different at all about me?"

Heddy took a good look at her mother. She had the same blonde hair, the same brown eyes, the same warm smile. She had just put on some weight, that was all.

"Nope," said Heddy. "You look the same, just a wee bit...(here Heddy tried to be diplomatic!) ...chubbier than usual. You have to watch those calories, Mom."

"I do intend to watch them, very carefully! These are rather special 'calories'. What kind do you prefer...boy-calories or girl-calories?"

Heddy looked at her mother again. She opened her mouth as if to say something, but no words came out. Suddenly, she understood. She jumped up and grabbed her mother's hands.

"Oh Mom! Are you serious? Really? I mean, do you *mean* it, or are you just teasing me?"

"I don't tease, especially about serious subjects," said Mrs. Levi with a very solemn look on her face.

"You mean we're going to have a baby? A *real* baby? Like Miriam and Rachel and Terry? Our own baby? Oh, how wonderful! I can't believe it! I'll be right back — I have to call Rachel!"

Heddy ran halfway out of the room and then did a turnabout. "When we will have it? The baby, I mean?"

"*B'ezrat Hashem* in another four months. Same month as your *bat mitzva.*"

"Four months? So long? Can't you hurry it up any? I can't wait that long!"

"Heddy, you are the funniest daughter I ever had!" said Mrs. Levi. Now she was really laughing hard.

Heddy was insulted. "I'm also the only daughter you ever had, but I don't understand why I'm so funny. I was only asking. But never mind — I know you can't hurry a baby up. It's just that four months is so long to wait."

"Why is it so long?" asked her mother. "While you're preparing for your *bat mitzva*, Dad and I will prepare for the baby. We'll all be very busy. The boys will be home and maybe we can even get Zeidy to come back for a visit. We've got lots to do before then."

Heddy suddenly remembered the long list of things she had to learn before her twelfth birthday. Zeidy had worked it all out with her before he left, and both Mom and Dad would help. There was no use having a party for her family and friends to celebrate if she herself wasn't properly prepared.

She had to learn all the basic *dinim* a young Jewess must know, now that she was becoming a young adult. She remembered how seriously Jeremy had thought about growing up and becoming a responsible, Jewish adult before his *bar mitzva*.

"Gee, I hope we have enough time to do all that preparing. A baby and a *bat mitzva* at the same time is an awful lot!"

"Everything in its own good time," said Mrs. Levi. "As long as we're preparing for a *simcha*, I have no complaints."

"Me neither," answered Heddy. She was already full of plans.

who's a goose?

The girls were in the den, preparing a surprise birthday party for their teacher Mrs. Kramer, but it sounded as though they were in the entire house. The sounds coming out of the den were rather loud.

"How many girls are in there?" Mr. Levi grumbled from behind his newspaper. "Fifty?"

"No. I think only five or six," said his wife.

"Five or six? That's impossible! It would take at least fifty to make that much noise! I'm going to see."

Mr. Levi strode into the den where he found Heddy with five friends. They were lying on the floor, hanging over the chairs, and skipping around the room. They were eating, drinking, laughing, giggling, singing, drawing, writing a play for Mrs. Kramer, telling jokes and talking — very loudly, all at once.

"Did you want something, Dad?" asked Heddy when she saw him.

"Just checking," said Mr. Levi. "It sounded as if

someone dropped off a truckload of wild geese and let them loose in the house. But the noise couldn't have been coming from here. All I see in the den are six lovely young swans."

"Oh! Were we making too much noise, Mr. Levi?" asked Rachel. "We're sorry! We'll try to be quieter!"

"My father says we *can't* be quiet. He says young girls are screechy by nature, so he doesn't fight it. He just uses earplugs when my friends come," Terry added.

"Nature develops and changes, you know," said Mr. Levi. "Haven't you heard the story about the ugly duckling who turned into a swan? I'm sure that with a little training, six screechy young geese could turn into lovely swans too! In fact, here are six tickets for the pool this afternoon. Why don't you all go for a swan-like swim? It could be the beginning of your metamorphosis and it will guarantee me a nice quiet afternoon."

"Thanks alot, Dad, but we have to finish this play!"

"Well, try and do it a *little* bit quieter, for my mental well-being, OK?"

"Sure, Mr. Levi! We wouldn't want to damage your mentality any!" said Aviva enthusiastically. The girls giggled.

"My mentality!" muttered Mr. Levi as he left the room. "Raising daughters damages the mentality, that's what!" But Sunday was finally over and a nice, quiet week stretched out in front of Mr. Levi. Or so he thought.

Monday evening, Mr. Levi had just come into the house from *maariv* when he was greeted with a loud "bang" from the second floor. Two minutes later, it was "boom". Then "clump". Every few minutes, something else seemed to fall.

"What's going on up there?" he asked his wife. "Can't a man have a little peace and quiet in his own home?"

"That's what they're practicing," said Mrs. Levi. "How to be peaceful and quiet. They're learning how to be young ladies. How to be polite, well behaved, graceful. Your calling them wild geese yesterday was the start of a new venture. Go on up and see!" Mrs. Levi laughed.

Mr. Levi walked up to Heddy's room. An official looking sign was taped onto the closed door:

G.T.S.
(GEESE TURNED SWANS)
A Developmental School
for Gracious Young Women

He knocked.

"G.T.S. Come in, please."

He opened the door and saw six girls sitting straight and high on the kitchen chairs. They all

had books on their head. Heddy rose slowly, careful not to drop her dictionary.

"Good evening, Father. Welcome to G.T.S. Would you care to sit down?"

"Not if it means I have to put a dictionary on my head, thank you," he answered. "Have you found a new way to study? Perhaps by osmosis? You put the book with the information on top of the head and it seeps in?"

"The books are to help us attain proper balance and grace, but you do have such a delightful sense of humor, sir," whispered Aviva.

"Beg your pardon," said Mr. Levi. "I didn't hear you. Could you speak up a bit?"

"You have such a delightful sense of humor, sir," she said again, this time in a louder voice.

"I do?"

"Yes indeed, and such splendid ideas. As you can see, we have taken your suggestion about turning into swans very seriously. We most definitely do not want to be geese, so we have initiated a course in gracious living. You'll notice, I spoke very softly now, didn't I?" she whispered again.

"Softly? Oh yes, yes. Very softly. I can't even make out what you're saying! Very soft indeed!"

Bang! Mr. Levi jumped. Aviva's encyclopedia had fallen down.

"Can't you learn gracious living at Kerem HaTorah??"

"Oh no, there's not enough time," answered Rachel. "There are so many other things to learn in school. That's why we need G.T.S. You see, sir, Heddy is the youngest, so she has a bit more time, but the rest of us are all *bat mitzva*, and the time has come for us to start acting like young ladies. Don't you agree?"

"Oh yes," said Mr. Levi. "Absolutely."

"And even I have to get started," said Heddy. "It's part of my *bat mitzva* preparation. We aren't going to run and jump and screech anymore. You'll like that, Father, " said Heddy.

"Dad," said Mr. Levi. "You never call me Father, only Dad."

"But Father is much more elegant."

"Could be, but I'm a Dad."

"You *were* a Dad until now, but you've developed and turned into a Father. And look how beautifully straight we're sitting and standing. And we're not going to chew any more gum."

"Or bust baloons!" giggled Rachel.

"Or slam doors," said Aviva.

"Or scream or run into the house," said Terry.

"We'll be perfect ladies!"

Bang! There went Rachel's book on birds. She bent down slowly, picked it up, and put it back on her head.

"We intend to hold classes for an hour a day for a week or two — until we are properly developed."

Bang!

"I see. Very nice. Good luck and all that!" Mr. Levi hurried out of the room and back to his wife in the kitchen.

"This is too much! I have to sit down! Where are the chairs? Oh, I forgot, the girls took them! When will this end? (Bang!) They're going to drive me crazy!" (Bang! Bang!)

"They'll get better at balancing and the books won't fall off so frequently," said Mrs. Levi. "And in a week they'll forget all about their Developmental School and just be themselves again. Meanwhile, enjoy the quiet." (Bang!)

"That's what's bothering me, the quiet! I don't mind the banging. I'm used to that. But all this whispering! I can't stand it. And Miriam, Heddy turned me into a Father! After eleven and a half years, I'm suddenly a Father! I'm not a Dad to my own daughter anymore."

"And I have become Mother. No more Mom. For a week or so."

"Do you think she'll start calling Zeidy 'Grandfather'? And will Jeremy become 'Jeremiah'? Why do you keep laughing?"

"I can't help it," said Mrs. Levi. "It's funny, and it's part of the process."

"What process?"

"You know — the metamorphosis — noisy young geese turning into lady-like swans! There's nothing you can do to hurry it up, so you might as well relax."

The book-banging and whispering continued. Then, as suddenly as it had started, it stopped. One day, Heddy zoomed into the house after school, slammed the door, threw her books on the table, hollered "Hi Dad! Hi Mom!", and ran up the stairs to her room. Two minutes later, she ran down. "What's to eat? I'm starving!"

Mr. Levi looked on in wonder. "What happened, Heddy?" he asked.

"What happened to what, Dad?" she answered with her mouth full.

"To the swans — you know — the gracious young women you want to become?"

"Oh that! The girls decided it was taking too long. Anyway, I think I'm too young to be a swan yet. Maybe we'll be swans on *Shabbat*. That's a good time for being genteel and gracious, don't you think? Gotta run now. I'm bringing Rachel her homework. She was sick today. I'll be back before supper. 'Bye!" She slammed the door and was gone.

"Thank goodness!" sighed Mr. Levi. "My goose is back!"

a piece of heaven

ב"ה

To my dear granddaughter Chedva, commonly known as Heddy – may she live to be one-hundred-and-twenty!

[Heddy loved the way Zeidy began his letters. He wrote such nice lengthy introductions and he always included a blessing or two!]

I was glad to hear you have started your bat mitzva preparations. Even though a girl is not called up to the Torah, her bat mitzva is no less important than a boy's. In fact, perhaps it's even more so, for the bat *– the girl – will one day be the* bayit *– the home. She will be the central pillar in a future Jewish family, and who wants a faulty central pillar in their house? I am sure you will master all of the material we discussed and that you will pass your "bat mitzva test" with flying colors!*

Yes, I will think about coming to visit for the baby and the bat mitzva, b'ezrat Hashem, *although I am never happy about leaving Israel – even for a short trip. It's not the travelling that bothers me.* Baruch Hashem, *I'm still young enough to sit in a plane. But I find it very difficult to leave here. I'm not sure you will understand why, but I shall try and explain.*

If someone who knew nothing about the Jews and the Torah and Eretz Yisrael *were to visit Israel, he would probably think that Israel is just another foreign country with a strange sounding language. At most, an interesting place to visit. Such a person could be compared to an ignorant man who finds a precious jewel but doesn't appreciate or understand its true value.*

A Jew who studies the Torah, however, knows that Eretz Yisrael *is not just another country. It is a very unique and important place – unlike any other in the world! – for it was created with very special ingredients.*

Of all the lands in the world, only this one contains the quality of kedusha, *of holiness; and only this one is blessed with so many* mitzvot! *You might say that* Eretz Yisrael *is the entrance to God's palace – a piece of heaven on earth. And He has given this "piece of heaven" to us, His children, the Jewish people.*

That's why, when I leave, even if it's only for a little while, I feel as though I am leaving something precious behind me – my place in the King's palace.

And it makes me as homesick and unhappy as you were the first year you went to summer camp. Do you remember how you complained that your head and your stomach hurt, and you had a heavy feeling in your chest every time you thought of home? That's exactly how I feel when I'm not here.

Which is why I would much rather wait for you to come and visit me, than for me to go and visit you. In fact, if your parents agree, your bat mitzva present from me will be a trip to Eretz Yisrael, *so you can add that to your other bat mitzva plans!*

["Oh!" cried Heddy. "That's wonderful!!!!"]

However, since your mother will obviously not be able to come when she has the baby, and since she wants me to be there for the kiddush *or the* brit, *I am considering coming to you for a month or so. As soon as I make a final decision, I will let your parents know. Danny will be returning then too, so I can come with him. We shall see.*

I was very happy to hear that your friend Tamara will soon be coming home from the hospital. Of course you should do whatever you can to help her and her family, but you mustn't be too hard on yourself either, Heddy. We all make mistakes and do silly things; that's why we have a Yom Kippur *every year!* Baruch Hashem, *in this case, no real harm was done and you'll have ample time to make amends and be a true friend to Tamara.*

Chazal *had may things to say about silence, and most of them were good! So it is most definitely worthwhile to practice keeping quiet, at least once in a while! And by the way, it gets easier with time. I know, because I've been practicing my entire life.*

[Now that was something interesting to think about: Zeidy having to practice keeping quiet! Heddy wouldn't have believed it if she hadn't read it with her own eyes!]

Send my warmest regards to your friends, especially to Rachel. Although she is your First Best Friend, I feel as though she is my Second Best Granddaughter!

Be well, study, and don't forget to listen to your parents – in between all the other important things you have to do.

May Hashem *watch you and keep you and guard you and fill your days with His blessings!*

From Your Zeidy Mattityahu,
With Love.

from Heddy with love

eddy licked the end
of her pen. "Ick!" she
sputtered. She got up
from her desk, walked over to the mirror on her
dresser, and stuck out her tongue.

"Blue, as usual. No wonder the girls say my
tongue is always blue when I write! I must
remember to stop doing that!"

Heddy sighed. There seemed to be so many things
to remember to do and to remember to stop doing.
She wondered if she'd ever have them all remembered and taken care of so she could forget about
them already!

"I'd better sit down and get this letter to Zeidy
finished," she thought, "before I forget that too!"

ב"ה

Dear Zeidy,

*I read your letter four times – once quickly, just to
see what you wrote; once to understand it better;
once to think about it; and once just to enjoy it – and
I think I can still get a good reading or two out of it.*

I have a lot to discuss with you, but I have to be careful with my tongue. Not because of saying anything wrong, but because of licking the pen. Dad says everytime I write you, my tongue is blue for days. I guess that's because I concentrate on the writing, not the licking.

I've been thinking about the year and it seems to me that it's a mixture of successes and failures. I kept away from chocolate although I never would have believed I could. What's most surprising of all is that I hardly even think of chocolate anymore and it doesn't bother me one bit when someone else eats it. Jeremy's carob candy wasn't very good, but I wanted to be polite, so I told him it was delicious. That was a mistake, because he kept sending me packages all year long. I had enough carob candy to plant a carob orchard! Mom finally told him not to send anymore.

I'm glad you appreciated the long underwear I sent you and I decided not to be embarrassed about it either, even if Rachel thought it was a funny gift. Isn't that a sign that I'm thinking independently and growing up?

Keeping the part of Nevuchadnezzar in the play and giving Snowball back to Mr. Sendler were both hard, but as Dad says, they were very "instructive experiences".

What was even harder was trying to keep quiet! At least Nevuchadnezzar and Snowball were over and done with, but not talking so much is never finished! Every time I remember to talk less, I think to myself, "Good for you Heddy Levi! You did it!" Then I promptly forget and I'm full of things to say all over again! The fact that you're still working on keeping quiet isn't very encouraging either. If you have trouble with it after seventy years, how can I ever hope to succeed? Mom says she has implicit faith in me, but she doesn't talk much, so I'm not sure she understands how hard it is.

I was going to babysit for the Twins during summer vacation. Now that I'm not sewing anymore (I decided I don't have the patience after all) I wanted to earn some money so I wouldn't have to ask Dad for a raise in my allowance. But with the baby coming, b'ezrat Hashem, I think Mom will appreciate some extra help in the house, so I told Mrs. Langsner I won't have time.

I can't tell you how excited I am about the baby. Just imagine – a whole, brand new human being! I keep wondering if it will be a He or a She. It doesn't really make any difference but it's fun thinking about each possibility. I don't think you love boy-babies any differently than you love girl-babies, do you?

I can't wait for everyone to be here – you, and the boys, and the baby! Our house will be beautifully full and noisy again. I try to fill the house up as much as I can by myself (and I guess I do keep the noise level up pretty well) but I'll be happy to have some help.

I learned most of my bat mitzva material and Mom and Dad test me on each section as I finish. They said I'm doing fine. They also said of course I could accept your bat mitzva gift of a trip to Israel, although not this summer, because of the baby. I'd like to come as soon as possible, but I don't mind waiting a bit. Mom needs me now, and that's important too, isn't it?

Besides, I need some time to prepare myself for coming to Eretz Yisrael, *and with all the other preparations going on around here, I can't do it properly right now. As soon as the baby is born and the bat mitzva is over, I plan to sit down and learn as much as I can about the subject. I'm hoping you'll help me while you're here. I'd hate to be like the ignorant man who found the precious gem but who didn't appreciate its value!*

Oof – I just licked the pen again! I think that's all for now. I want to wash my tongue off before the ink dries.

Hurry and come. I'm counting the weeks!

From your Loving and First and Very Own
Granddaughter Heddy,
With Love.

P.S. May Hashem *watch you and keep you and guard you and fill your days with His blessings too!*

Glossary of Hebrew and Yiddish Words

BAR MITZVA: a Jewish boy who, at age 13, becomes obligated to perform the commandments

BAT MITZVA: a Jewish girl who, at age 12, becomes obligated to perform the commandments

BARUCH HASHEM: Thank God!

BEIT HAMIKDASH: the Holy Temple which was in Jerusalem

BENTCH: saying the prayer after a meal (Yiddish)

B'EZRAT HASHEM: with God's help

BIKKUR CHOLIM: visiting the sick

BIRKAT HAMAZON: the prayer after eating a meal

BRACHA: a blessing

BRIT: the circumcision and name-giving ceremony on the eighth day after the birth of Jewish boys

CHAZAL: Chachameynu, Zichronam Livracha: Our Rabbis, may their memory serve as a blessing

CHUMASH: The Five Books of Moses

DAVEN, DAVENING: to pray (Yiddish)

DIKDUK: Hebrew grammar

DINIM: laws

ERETZ YISRAEL: The Land of Israel

GAM ZU LETOVA: This, too, is good.

GEMILLAT CHESED: doing good deeds

HASHEM: God

KEDUSHA: holiness

KIBUD AV: the commandment to honor your father

KIDDUSH: the Sabbath blessing over wine; also refers to the celebration for any happy event — births, bar or bat mitzvas, engagements, and the naming of a girl — which is made after the Shabbat morning "kiddush"

KIPPA: small, round skullcap worn by Jewish men and boys

LASHON HARA: gossip

MAARIV: the evening prayer

MINYAN: the ten men needed for communal prayer

MITZVA, MITZVOT: commandment, commandments

MOSHE RABBEINU: Moses our teacher

MOTZAI SHABBAT: the end of the Sabbath; Saturday night after the appearance of three stars in the sky

NEVUCHADNEZZAR: Nebuchadnezzar, king of Babylonia, who conquered Jerusalem and destroyed the First Temple

PESACH: the holiday of Passover

RAV: rabbi (teacher)

REFUAH SHLEYMA: a full recovery from sickness

ROSH CHODESH: the beginning of the Hebrew month

SEFER, SEFARIM: book, books; here referring specifically to books of Jewish learning

SHABBOS, SHABBAT: the Sabbath

SHEVA BRACHOT: seven blessings made in honor of a bride and groom; the seven nights of celebration after the marriage when these blessings are repeated

SHUL: synagogue (Yiddish)

SIMCHA: a celebration; a happy event

TALMID CHACHAM: a scholar

TEHILLIM: King David's Book of Psalms

TZAAR BAAL CHAYIM: the prohibition against harming animals

TZEDAKA: charity

YESHIVA: a school where the Talmud is studied; nowadays, also refers to Jewish day-schools

ZEIDY: grandfather (Yiddish)

ZEMIROT: the songs sung after the Sabbath meals

Other Feldheim Young Readers Division books by YAFFA GANZ: